RAINBOOTS

BLOOMSBURY EDUCATION
Bloomsbury Publishing Plc
50 Bedford Square, London, WC1B 3DP, UK

BLOOMSBURY, BLOOMSBURY EDUCATION and the Diana logo
are trademarks of Bloomsbury Publishing Plc

First published in Great Britain 2012 by A & C Black, an imprint of Bloomsbury Publishing Plc
This edition published in Great Britain 2019 by Bloomsbury Publishing Plc

A catalogue record for this book is available from the British Library

ISBN: PB: 978-1-4729-6079-5; ePDF: 978-1-4729-6078-8; ePub: 978-1-4729-6077-1

2 4 6 8 10 9 7 5 3 1

Typeset by Integra Software Services Pvt. Ltd.
Printed and bound in China by Leo Paper Products

To find out more about our authors and books visit
www.bloomsbury.com and sign up for our newsletters

recommended by

www.catchup.org

Catch Up is a not-for-profit charity which aims to address the problem of
underachievement that has its roots in literacy and numeracy difficulties.

CHRIS POWLING
RAINBOW
BOOTS

ILLUSTRATED BY

JIM FIELD

BLOOMSBURY EDUCATION

LONDON OXFORD NEW YORK NEW DELHI SYDNEY

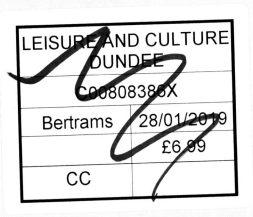

CONTENTS

Chapter One

The Coolest Boots

Rainbow Boots, they were called. They had big thick soles, thin flat laces and were so flashy they made you blink. It was as if somebody had dipped them in a tin of rainbow paint.

Denzil really wanted a pair of Rainbow Boots.

But his mum said, "No! Rainbow Boots are a real waste of money!"

"All the other kids have got them!" Denzil wailed.

"**All** the other kids?" said Mum.

"Well, all the cool kids..." said Denzil.

"It's time you grew up," Mum said. "Who cares about stuff that's trendy today and past its sell-by date tomorrow?"

"Stevie Glossop thinks Rainbow Boots are cool, and he plays football for England!" said Denzil crossly. "He makes adverts for Rainbow Boots on TV!"

"I bet they pay him loads of cash,"
Mum said.

"Yes, they do!" said Denzil.

Mum laughed and went on reading her book. Being cool didn't matter a bit to her. But it mattered a lot to Denzil.

Chapter Two

On Order

It mattered a lot to the other kids, too.

Later that day, a girl called Lorna came up to Denzil.

"Oh, poor you," she said to Denzil. "You **still** don't have any Rainbow Boots. Aren't you fed up with those scruffy old trainers?"

"My Rainbow Boots are on order," said Denzil, quickly.

"On order?" Lorna asked. "What do you mean?"

"Hand-made just for me," Denzil said. "My boots will be **customised**. Not like yours, Lorna. Your Rainbow Boots are the same as everybody else's. My boots will be special."

Lorna gave Denzil a sly look.

"That's great, Denzil!" she said. "Shall I tell all the other kids? I bet they'd love to hear about the special, hand-made, customised Rainbow Boots you've got on order!"

"Go on then," said Denzil.

Lorna ran off, giggling.

Denzil heard a loud groan. It was Nadeem, his best friend.

"You're such a liar," Nadeem said to Denzil. "You haven't got a pair of special, hand-made customised Rainbow Boots on order. You haven't got *any* Rainbow Boots on order. You made it all up!"

Denzil looked down at his trainers.

Lorna was right. They were old and scruffy. They were creased from too much football in the street. They weren't cool.

Denzil gave a shrug.

"OK," he said. "So I made it all up. The other kids don't know that, do they?"

"Not yet," said Nadeem, gloomily. "But how long before they find out?"

Chapter Three

Gossip

Soon almost everyone in the school was talking about the Rainbow Boots Denzil had on order. At lunchtime, kids crowded round him.

"Will your boots really be hand-made?"
someone asked.

"Every stitch," said Denzil.

"And customised?" added another kid.

Denzil nodded. "You bet."

"You mean, even better than Stevie Glossop's Rainbow Boots on TV?" called a third kid.

"Much better," said Denzil.

"So when do we get to see them?" asked the first kid.

This was the killer question. Denzil was thinking hard as he stared up at the smart green roof of the school's new assembly hall.

"Who knows?" he said, at last. "It takes weeks to make Rainbow Boots like mine. If you rush them they could be ruined."

Even Lorna was impressed.

"Nice one, Denzil," she said. "You've got all the kids hooked now. They can't wait to see your boots."

"No problem," Denzil said.

"No problem?" exclaimed Nadeem on the way home. "These special, hand-made, customised boots of yours don't exist. **That's** the problem!"

"Look," said Denzil. "I'll get it sorted, OK?"

"How?" asked Nadeem.

Denzil shook his head. He had no idea how. But a clever kid like him was bound to think of something.

Well, wasn't he?

Chapter Four

A Present for Nadeem

Next morning, Nadeem was waiting at Denzil's front gate. He had a funny look on his face.

"What's up?" Denzil asked.

Nadeem opened the fancy plastic bag he'd been holding behind his back.

Inside it was a pair of Rainbow Boots. They had big thick soles, thin flat laces, and were so flashy they made you blink.

"Dad bought them for me," said Nadeem. "As an early birthday present."

"Who needs a best friend like you?" Denzil snapped.

They didn't say a word to each other all the way to school.

The bell for going-in was already ringing when they got there.

The first kid they met was Lorna. Her eyes lit up when she saw Nadeem's bag.

"Is that a pair of Rainbow Boots?" she asked.

"Yes. They're an early birthday present," said Nadeem.

"Great!" said Lorna.

Then she turned to Denzil. "So where are *your* boots? They're still being customised, I suppose?"

"No," said Denzil.

"No?" said Lorna in surprise.

"My Rainbow Boots arrived by the same post as Nadeem's," Denzil told her. "But I sent them back."

"You sent them back?" said Lorna.

"I know a rush-job when I see it, Lorna. The boots weren't flashy enough. So I told the boot-makers to rip them apart and start all over again."

And Denzil marched off into school. Nadeem could hardly believe his ears.

"Another lie?" he said to himself. "Denzil's getting worse and worse!"

Chapter Five

Captain of England

The news went round the school like wildfire.
Denzil had sent back his customised Rainbow
Boots! And all because they were a rush-job!

"He's so cool!" most of the kids gasped.

"That's if you think it's true," Lorna sniffed. "We've only got Denzil's word for it."

"You mean he's telling lies?" asked a kid.

Lorna scratched her head. "Nah," she said, after a while. "Not even Denzil would dare do that."

That morning, in assembly, there were Rainbow Boots everywhere. They even got a smile from the headteacher, Miss Hooper.

"I'm not very fond of Rainbow Boots," she said. "But today I'm really glad to see them."

She went on, "Next week is the Grand Opening of our brand-new school hall. I've been waiting for someone special to come and cut the tape for us. Can you guess who I've asked to do it?"

All the kids shook their heads.

Miss Hooper's eyes twinkled.

"Our visitor is rather keen on Rainbow Boots, I'm told," Miss Hooper said. "He's Stevie Glossop – the captain of England's football team. And today he said yes to my invitation!"

Nobody spoke. They were too stunned.

The rest of the assembly passed in a daze. So did the rest of the day.

When the bell rang for home-time, everybody was still in a happy dream. They were all thinking about Stevie Glossop. The captain of England was coming to their school!

At the school gate, Denzil and Nadeem bumped into Lorna.

"Oh, Denzil," she said, sweetly. "I've got good news."

"What?" asked Denzil.

"I told Miss Hooper about your customised Rainbow Boots," Lorna said. "I asked her if you could show them to Stevie Glossop."

"What did she say?" said Denzil.

"Miss Hooper thought it was a great idea!" said Lorna. "She said she would call you up on stage so everyone can see them!"

"On stage?" said Denzil. His voice sounded odd. "In assembly?"

The two boys stared at Lorna in horror. She smiled and turned away.

Her Rainbow Boots were just like everyone else's boots. But they still looked flashy as she walked along the pavement.

Chapter Six

Denzil's Big Idea

The boys went to Nadeem's house and sat in his bedroom. They were trying to think what to do.

Denzil was in a panic now. He stared at Nadeem's birthday Rainbow Boots. If only he had his own Rainbow Boots!

Then Denzil blinked.

He'd just had an idea... a terrific idea!

"Er... Nadeem," he said. "Are you really my very best friend?"

Nadeem had heard that voice before. Denzil always talked like that when he wanted something badly.

The trouble was, Nadeem could never say no.

It was just the same this time.

"Look," said Denzil over and over again. "I only want to **borrow** your boots, OK? You can have them back after Stevie Glossop's visit. We'll customise them for the assembly then un-do the customising later so they look like all the other Rainbow Boots."

"What if we can't un-do it?" asked Nadeem. "What if my Rainbow Boots get ruined?"

"What harm can we do with a bit of paint and glue?" asked Denzil.

"Well..." said Nadeem.

"It'll be easy, I promise you."

Nadeem gave in. "OK, then."

To Nadeem's surprise, it really was easy.

They traced patterns on the heels and toes with magic markers.

They nicked some wings from a Viking helmet that belonged to Nadeem's little brother.

They stuck bike reflectors on the insteps to make them glow in the dark.

Soon Nadeem's boots were as close to customised as they could get.

Denzil was grinning from ear to ear as he tried them on.

"Better than Stevie Glossop's boots on TV," he said.

Nadeem looked down at his messy old trainers.

"And I'm stuck with these," he said. "I'll be the only kid in the hall who isn't wearing Rainbow Boots!"

"You did it for me, Nadeem," said Denzil, smugly. "That's why you're my very best mate."

There was no answer to that.

Chapter Seven

In Assembly

Stevie Glossop's visit was a big success.

"Magic!" he said when he looked in the classrooms.

"Great!" he said when he saw the display work.

"Cool!" he said when he cut the tape across the door to the new school hall.

"Wow!" he said when he saw all the kids in their Rainbow Boots.

"Here's another surprise!" said Miss Hooper.

She pressed a hidden button. The stage-curtains opened and the spot-lights went on. And there was Denzil.

He stood on one leg like a stork and lifted
one of his boots. He shook it about in the air
so everybody could see it. Then he switched to
the other boot.

"I'm over the moon!" Stevie gasped. "Those are much more flashy than my Rainbow Boots! They must have been – "

"CUSTOMISED!" all the kids yelled.

The cheering went on and on.

Miss Hooper took ages to hush everyone up. "Don't you want to hear Stevie's speech?" she shouted.

"Speech?" said Stevie.

His face was as white as a penalty spot.

"I'm rubbish at speeches," he said. "They scare me stiff."

Miss Hooper looked at him in dismay.

So did everyone else in the hall. It was as if the captain of England had just missed an open goal.

Chapter Eight

Trainer Talk

"I'm no good with words," said Stevie. "I do my best talking with my feet. Shall I show you what I mean?"

"Yes, please!" said Miss Hooper.

"I need a 50p coin," said Stevie. "And a pair of trainers, size 8."

"Here's the coin," Miss Hooper said. "But can't you use your Rainbow Boots?"

"Rainbow Boots are great fun," Stevie said. "But you can't play football in them. The soles are much too thick and the laces are much too thin. I just need a pair of old trainers. Can anybody here lend me a pair?"

"Nadeem's wearing trainers!" Lorna called.

"And he's got huge feet!"

"May I try them out, Nadeem?" Stevie
asked.

"OK…" said Nadeem.

Stevie took a good long look at Nadeem's trainers. Nadeem's face went bright red. His trainers looked more scruffy than ever.

But Stevie grinned as he put them on. "They're perfect!" he said.

He span the 50p coin in the air. It landed flat on his forehead, slid down his nose and dropped onto his knee. Then he flicked it from one trainer to the other.

It was the best game of Keepsie-Upsie they'd ever seen. The coin flipped up and down his body from head to toe.

Stevie finished the show by lobbing the 50p into the top pocket of his England blazer.

"Anybody can do it," he said. "All you need is practice and a pair of trainers just like these. Shall I sign my name on them, Nadeem?"

Nadeem nodded.

He could hardly speak, he felt so proud.

Quickly, he sneaked a look behind him. Denzil was sitting on stage cross-legged to hide what he had on his feet.

Rainbow Boots had suddenly lost their coolness – even if they *had* been customised. By tomorrow, every kid in the school would be playing Keepsie-Upsie with a 50p coin and a pair of old trainers.

Nadeem smiled as he slipped his own trainers back on – the ones with Stevie Glossop's name on them.

He felt a bit sorry for Denzil.

But only a bit.

Bonus Bits!

Quiz Time

How much can you remember about the story? Look back at the text to help if you need to. There are answers at the end (but no peeking before you finish!)

1. What lie does Denzil tell Lorna?

  A His boots have arrived and are customised.

  B His boots are on order and customised.

  C His boots are normal Rainbow Boots.

2. What colour is the roof of the new school assembly hall?

  A blue

  B black

  C green

3. Why does Denzil get upset with Nadeem?

  A Nadeem has a new pair of Rainbow boots

  B Nadeem has broken his Rainbow boots

  C Nadeem breaks Denzil's new trainers

4. What did they use from Nadeem's little brother to customise the boots?

  A horns from a Viking helmet

  B wings from a Viking helmet

  C wings from a racing outfit

5. What did Stevie ask for when on stage?

  A 50p coin and a pair of size 8 trainers

  B 50p coin and a pair of size 6 trainers

  C £1 coin and a pair of size 8 trainers

6. Where did the coin go at the end of the show?

  A Behind Stevie's ear

  B In Stevie's top pocket

  C Behind Nadeem's ear

WHAT NEXT?

Have a think about these questions after reading this story:

- How does Nadeem feel at the beginning, middle and end of the story?
- How do you think Denzil feels at the end of the story?
- Have you ever really wanted a particular item that is fashionable? What was it? Did you get it?

ANSWERS to QUIZ TIME

1B, 2D, 3A, 4C, 5A, 6B